CatKid

A Purrfect Princess

Hi! My name is CatKid.

That means I'm one whole-half cat and one whole-half kid. It also means I'm two full halves cute! Most people have never seen a half-cat, half-kid before. Know why? Because I'm special, that's why!

CatKid

A Purrfect Princess

Brian James

illustrated by
Ned Woodman

A
LITTLE APPLE
PAPERBACK

SCHOLASTIC INC.
New York Toronto London Auckland Sydney
Mexico City New Delhi Hong Kong Buenos Aires

No part of this publication may be reproduced, stored in a retrieval system, or transmitted in any form or by any means, electronic, mechanical, photocopying, recording, or otherwise, without written permission of the publisher. For information regarding permission, write to Scholastic Inc., Attention: Permissions Department, 557 Broadway, New York, NY 10012.

ISBN-13: 978-0-439-88856-1
ISBN-10: 0-439-88856-5

Text copyright © 2007 by Brian James. All rights reserved. Published by Scholastic Inc. SCHOLASTIC and associated logos are trademarks and/or registered trademarks of Scholastic Inc.

Book design by Tim Hall

12 11 10 9 8 7 6 5 4 3 2 1   7 8 9 10 11 12/0
40
Printed in the U.S.A.
First printing, November 2007

For my second grade teacher, Mrs. Donlin

Chapter 1:

One Special Surprise!

I, CatKid, cross my arms and make a very big huff once our class finishes saying the Pledge. Then I make an extra-grumpy face. My dad calls that *being steamed.* He says that's because he can see steam coming out of my ears.

Only know what?

Nothing ever comes out of my ears, that's what! I know because I've checked.

I check now, too. I uncross my arms and cover my ears with my hands. No steam. But that doesn't mean I'm not grumpy, so I go right back to crossing my arms.

It's all Shelly's fault!

Shelly is the bossiest girl in my whole entire second-grade class. Plus, she's a meanie.

"Hey Dumb Ears, it's *indivisible*, not *INVISIBLE!*" she shouts at me when our class is walking over to the story-time rug. That's what gets me steamed.

Some of the kids in my class start to laugh, but I don't think it's funny, not even one bit.

"Yeah, only it's called a mistake, so there!" I say back at her. Then I double cross my arms and make a double huff.

Then there's a tug on my tail and I spin around. Billy is standing there pointing at me. Billy is a big bully. He's always pulling my tail and saying stinky things to me. That means me and Billy are NOT friends.

"Even kindergarten babies know the words to the Pledge," he teases.

That makes me super steamy.

"I, CatKid, am NOT a baby!" I holler at his face.

Mrs. Sparrow comes right over to us. She doesn't like shouting, so I quickly cover my mouth with both hands. I don't want to get my name on the board or even worse, sent to the principal's office.

I don't know what happens in that office, but it can't be good! Even the fifth graders are afraid of being sent there, so it must be even scarier than the haunted house at the amusement park. And *that* haunted place scares the pants off me!

I don't want my pants to be scared off in school.

"I'm sorry for shouting," I mumble,

because saying sorry is a good way to stay out of trouble.

And guess what?

It works, that's what!

Mrs. Sparrow isn't mad. She pats me on the head and even scratches me behind my ears. I just love that scratching stuff, and it makes me go all purry. "Take a seat kids. I have a special announcement," she says.

"Special announcement" is a fancy way of saying she has a surprise. It makes me forget all about Billy being rotten.

I really love surprises! My favorite kinds of surprises are surprise cookies.

Since we're not really allowed to eat in class, Mrs. Sparrow probably has some other kind of surprise, and I, CatKid, can't wait to find out what it is. I race to the spot on the rug next to Maddie. Maddie is my bestest friend in the whole entire universe. That means I like her a lot.

I'm still purring when I sit down, and that makes Maddie giggle. "You sound a little bit like a refrigerator," she laughs.

"Or like a race car," Preston says. Preston is my third best friend, right after Kendra.

"Yeah, or like a lion," I say proudly.

"Whatever you sound like, it's gross," Shelly says. Then she rolls her eyes and scoots away. "They shouldn't let cats in school, anyway," she says.

"Only know what? I'm only half cat!" I say. I wait for her to turn her head around. Then I stick out my tongue at her. I have to stick up for my cat half, it's one of my favorite halves.

Maddie gives me the thumbs-up. She likes my cat half just as much as I do.

"Okay class, settle down," Mrs. Sparrow says. We all go whispery and then quiet. Then Mrs. Sparrow says she's not going to read a story today.

At first, I moan and groan because story time is one of my favorite subjects. If that's Mrs. Sparrow's surprise, then I'm starting to think it's the worst surprise ever. It's even stinkier than the surprises Maddie's baby brother leaves in his diaper!

But Mrs. Sparrow is one tricky teacher. Just then she tells us that the no-story thingy isn't the special announcement.

"Phew, that was close," I whisper to Maddie.

Maddie nods her head.

"As you know, every year one second-grade class is picked to put on a play for the entire school," Mrs. Sparrow tells us.

My ears perk up. That sure is a special announcement because I, CatKid, had never heard about any school play before. I raise my hand and stand up. "I didn't know that," I say.

"Me, either," Kendra says. Then she raises her hand and stands up, too.

"I knew it," Bradley says.

I roll my eyes. Bradley knows *everything*! Or at least he thinks he does because he's a smarty pants.

Mrs. Sparrow holds her hand up like a stop sign. That sign is for me and Kendra to sit down. It means she's not done with the surprise.

"I spoke to Principal Wheeler this morning," she says. "He said that our class has been chosen to put on this year's play!"

I spring right back up!

So does every other kid in my class. We all shout and dance around, and Mrs. Sparrow doesn't even tell us to stop. We make so much noise that Mrs. Andrews, the teacher next door, pokes her head in to see if everything is okay.

Finally, Mrs. Sparrow makes a *shhhhh* noise and tells us all to sit down again. "The first thing we need to do is decide which play we want to perform," she says once we get quiet.

All at once, every kid in my class shouts out the name of a play. Only, know what?

Every kid shouts out the name of a *different* play, that's what!

"I have a funny feeling this play business is going to be trouble," Maddie
whispers to me.

I look around.

Everybody looks steamed.

Everybody wants their play to be picked.

"Yeah, big trouble," I whisper back.

Chapter 2:

Fair and Square

"Ninjas From Space!" Billy says when Mrs. Sparrow calls on him. Then he makes karate noises and pretends to karate chop my tail.

"That's not even a real play," I tell him.

"So?" he says.

"So, you can't say it then," I tell him. That's what Mrs. Sparrow calls *debating*. We are debating what play our class should put on for the school.

"Can, too!" Billy shouts.

I'm just about to spin around on the story-time rug and shout back when Mrs.

Sparrow says, "Billy, we have to suggest real plays."

That's exactly what I said, only Mrs. Sparrow says it in teacher words. I could turn around and tell Billy that I told him so, but I don't. That's called being the bigger cat. And besides, it's my turn to suggest a play.

I jump straight up and raise my hand.

"The Little Mermaid!" I shout.

Then I smile my whiskers because I like that play. That's because mermaids are like me: one whole-half kid and one whole-half something else. Only their other half is a fish half. And I, CatKid, love fish!

I love fish for breakfast.

I love fish for lunch.

I love fish for snack time.

And I love, love, LOVE fish for dinner! Especially fish on a stick. Those fish sticks are super yummy!

But I also like the not-food kind of fish, too. Like my pet goldfish that live at Maddie's house. I would never ever want to eat them. Mermaids are that kind of fish, too.

"But some of *The Little Mermaid* takes place under water," Bradley says.

"So?" I say.

"So how are we going to do that?" he asks.

I scratch my head and think.

"Got it!" I say. "First, we get a really giant fish tank. Next, we take a deep breath like this . . ." Then I take a deep breath and hold it to show him what I mean.

Mrs. Sparrow tells me to stop holding my breath. Then she says that we don't need a tank. "A play is all about pretending," she says. "We can pretend we are under water."

I make a frown. I like my idea better. Maybe I can try it out in the bathtub when I get home.

Then I raise my hand. "Since we can't have it under water, can I change my answer to *Snow White*?" I ask, because *Snow White* is my second-favorite play. Also, zero parts of *Snow White* take place under water.

Mrs. Sparrow makes a funny breathing noise. It's the same noise my mom makes when I change my mind about what kind of cookies I want after she's already started to make them. But it's not my fault. I can't help it if cats are finicky.

"Okay, CatKid," Mrs. Sparrow says. Then she crosses *The Little Mermaid* off the list and writes *Snow White*.

The next turn is Maddie's turn.

Maddie puts her finger to her chin. That's what she does when she's thinking. Then she points her finger in the air. That means she's thought of something.

"*Annie!*" she says. "My mom and dad took me to see that play once." Then she starts to sing at the top of her lungs.

"That sounds like a girl play," Billy says.

"Yeah, well there are twelve girls in our class and only nine boys, so that only makes sense!" Maddie says.

"Thank you, Maddie, that's a very good suggestion," Mrs. Sparrow says. "However, *Annie* is a musical, and we don't have a band to play music."

"Oh," Maddie says. "Then can I change my answer to *Snow White*, too?"

I smile my whiskers at Maddie. "That's a good answer," I whisper.

Next, Mrs. Sparrow calls on Shelly. That's what I call *one stinky turn*.

"I think it should be *Cinderella*," Shelly says. "It's the best play." Then she lifts her nose in the air and makes a snotty face.

"Yeah, only I don't even like *Cinderella*," I tell her. "Those sisters are real meanies."

"Then there's a perfect part for you!" Shelly says.

That makes me hiss under my breath. "That shows what you know!" I say back at her. "If I were a sister, I wouldn't even be the littlest bit mean."

Maddie leans over and whispers in my ear. "If we did *Cinderella*, Shelly could be the wicked stepmother. That's because they're both the meanest."

I go all giggly thinking about that. Shelly would make a good wicked anything.

"I heard you," Shelly says. "And, anyway, I would play the part of Cinderella, because I'm the most like a princess."

That's when Mrs. Sparrow tells us that we will have to try out for parts, no matter which play we pick. The whole class makes *oooohhhhs* and *aaaahhhhs* because tryouts are very grown-up.

Then Mrs. Sparrow finishes asking each kid to name a play. She writes down only the real plays. She doesn't write down the plays that are really only the names of TV shows. That means there are a total of five plays to pick from.

1. *Beauty and the Beast*
2. *Snow White*
3. *Peter Pan*
4. *Jack and the Beanstalk*
5. *Cinderella*

"Okay, we will take a vote to see which one wins," Mrs. Sparrow says. She says voting equals fair. "I will read off a name

BEAUTY AND THE BEAST

2. SNOW WHITE

3. PETER PAN

ACK AND THE BEANSTALK

5. CINDERELL

and I want you to raise your hand if that's the play you want."

Then she reads the first name and I look around. I don't like that play one bit. That's because Billy says I would have to be the beast. That makes me growl because everyone knows the beast is a boy and I, CatKid, will never ever play a boy!

I count the hands in the air. *Beauty and the Beast* gets three votes.

Next is *Snow White*. It gets seven votes!

"We're in first place," I tell Maddie.

I try my best to keep track, but there are so many votes that I lose count. So when Mrs. Sparrow is ready to read the name of the winner, I have a hard time keeping still.

"I've counted all the votes," Mrs. Sparrow says, "And the winner is . . . *Snow White* by one vote."

"YIPPY!" I shout. *Snow White* is the winner by a whisker!

Some of the boys in my class make icky noises.

"Why do we have to do a princess play?" Bradley says. "It's not fair."

"Only it is fair," I say to him. "We voted and voting is fair and square."

Mrs. Sparrow agrees. "Besides, there

are a lot of roles that aren't princess roles."

"Like the dwarves!" Preston shouts. Then our class goes all giggly thinking about those funny dwarves.

"That's right," Mrs. Sparrow says. Then she tells us that we will try out for parts tomorrow. "So think about which part you might want," she says.

Only know what?

I don't have to think about it because I already know which part I want. I want to be Snow White. And I'm going to practice all night to make sure I get the part.

Chapter 3:

Practice Makes Perfect

That night after dinner, I race up the stairs to my room. Then I look through my closet for my princess dress. I look under my stuffed animals and behind the pile of games.

I can't find it anywhere!

So I race over to my door and open it. "MOM!" I shout. "WHERE'S MY PRINCESS DRESS?"

That's the best way to find something that is missing in my house.

My mom comes up the stairs to my room. Then she goes over to my dresser

and opens the bottom drawer. "I think
it's in here," she says.

I make a face and scratch my head. I
NEVER open that drawer. It is filled with
old itchy sweaters that I don't like.

Only guess what?

My princess dress is right there on top,
that's what!

"Thank you! Thank
you! THANK YOU!"
I shout and
give my mom a
big hug.
"You're the
best finder in
the whole
wide world."

My mom laughs. "You're welcome,
kitten."

I stop my hug right then.

"Only know what?" I say. "I'm not
a kitten anymore!" Then I make my

ears droopy so that she knows I mean business.

"Yes, yes. I'm sorry," my mom says. "You're a full-grown CatKid, I forgot."

"That's okay," I tell her. Then I smile my whiskers because my mom is one silly mom. I don't know how she always forgets about that kitten stuff but remembers things like where my princess dress is hiding.

I put on that dress right over my clothes. Then I look in the mirror. I look just like a princess! A *purr*-fect princess!

My mom agrees. "I almost forgot you had that dress," she says. "You haven't worn it in so long."

I cross my arms and make a frown.

"Yeah, only I'm not playing," I tell her. "I'm practicing for our class play. We're doing *Snow White*, and I want to be Snow White!"

"Oh?" my mom says. "That sounds important."

"It is." I nod. "It's important business."

"Then I'd better let you practice," she says. Then she looks around at my messy room. "You know, Snow White is very tidy. Perhaps you should practice by straightening up."

I scratch my head and think about that.

Maybe it's not such a bad idea. If I want to get the star role, I need to be prepared for anything! That's a cat-fact.

I get to work right away.

Mrs. Sparrow gave us all a copy of the play. I pull it out of my backpack. Then I practice talking like Snow White. And I practice walking like Snow White. I even practice straightening up like Snow White. By the time my dad knocks on my door to tell me it's bedtime, I feel like I really am Snow White!

My dad says he's real proud of me for practicing. My tail goes all twitchy then because I like that *proud-of-me* stuff.

"Do you think I'll get the part?" I ask him.

"I don't know," he says. "But even if you don't, you'll always be my princess."

I give him a big hug for that.

He gives me a hug right back. Then he says that even princesses have bedtimes.

"But can't a princess change her bed-time?" I ask. "After all, a princess is the boss of the castle."

"Not this castle," my dad says with a smile.

Then he says that any princess that isn't in bed in ten minutes will get tickled. My eyes go all wide and I leap up in the air.

I, CatKid, do NOT like tickles!

So, I run into the bathroom and start brushing my teeth. Then I change into my pajamas and hop into bed. Besides, if I'm going to get that part, I need my beauty sleep.

Chapter 4:

Trying Your Bestest

I, CatKid, can't stand still. That's because our class is getting ready for our tryouts. I'm so excited that I want to run all over the place. That's what my mom calls *being frisky*.

But I only have to run to one place because Mrs. Sparrow put up signs in our classroom. Each sign has the name of a different part written on it.

"Class, I want you to go stand by the sign with the part you want to try out for," she tells us.

I leap right out of my desk. Then I grab

Maddie's hand. "Come on Maddie, let's go to the Snow White sign," I say.

"Know what?" Maddie says. "I want to be one of the dwarves."

I put my ears way back. I can't believe what I'm hearing. "Why?" I ask.

"Because Snow White has a lot of words to say," Maddie says. Then she leans over and whispers in my ear. "And don't tell anyone, but sometimes I get stage fright."

I cover my mouth. Then I pretend to zip my lips closed. "Don't worry," I say. "I'll keep it our secret!"

"Thanks," Maddie says.

"Sure thing. That's what best friends

do," I say. "And also, you're always happy just like one of those dwarves. So I think you'll be perfect for that part," I tell her.

Then I cross my fingers for her and Maddie crosses her fingers for me, too.

I go over to the Snow White sign. There are the most kids by that sign. There are six girls waiting there. That's what I, CatKid, call a lot of competition.

"Oh great, you're trying out?" Shelly says to me. "Shouldn't you try out for the grouchy dwarf?"

I make a growly face at her. But then I stop right away, because that growly face is sort of like a grumpy face. Making a grumpy face would mean Shelly is right. I do NOT want her to be right.

"Don't listen to her," Kendra says. Kendra is trying out for the part of Snow White, too. Only Kendra is *friendly* competition and Shelly is stinky competition.

"Yeah, anyway she should try out for Snotty Dwarf," I say.

That makes all the other Snow Whites giggle. Except Shelly.

"That's not even one of the dwarves, so there!" Shelly says.

"Only I knew that already," I say. "I was just acting."

Shelly rolls her eyes but doesn't say anything. That's because Mrs. Sparrow says it's time to start the tryouts.

"We'll start with the role of Prince Charming," she says.

There are four boys trying out for that part.

"I hope Preston gets that part," I whisper to Kendra. "I wouldn't want any of those other boys to be the prince."

She nods. "Especially not Billy," she says.

Then we both hold our noses and stick out our tongues like we smell something stinky. That means we both think Billy would make an icky prince.

Each boy takes a turn reading a part. I try my best not to giggle, but it's not easy. It's pretty funny watching them act like princes. Plus, they had to say lines about true love, and true love is giggly stuff.

The next part is the part of the Wicked Queen. Only our class gets to skip that part because not even one kid tries out for it. Nobody wants to be that mean even for pretend.

Mrs. Sparrow says it's one of the most important roles. "Doesn't anybody want to try it?" she asks.

We all shake our heads.

Mrs. Sparrow makes a frown. It's the same frown the lunch lady makes when I accidentally throw food at Billy on purpose. "I'm disappointed," Mrs. Sparrow says, just like the lunch lady does. "I'll have to assign the role to someone. But whoever gets that role should be proud," she says.

I, CatKid, am not so sure. I would rather be that dwarf who sleeps all the time than the Wicked Queen because I don't like mean queens one bit!

Then I forget all about the Queen business because the next is the best part. That's because Mrs. Sparrow says it's time for the Snow White tryouts.

Kendra goes first.

"Good luck," I say.

Only it doesn't work, because she forgets all her lines. Then Lauren goes and she forgets her lines, too. In fact, every girl before me forgets most of her lines and that makes me extra glad I practiced so much.

"Okay CatKid, it's your turn," Mrs. Sparrow says.

I take a deep breath. Then I stand in front of the class and start my tryout.

I start by straightening up Mrs. Sparrow's desk. "From the look of this place, it belongs to seven untidy little children," I say because that's one of the lines.

I see Maddie and she gives me the thumbs-up. That means I'm doing a good job.

And when I finish, the whole class claps. That means I did a really, really good job.

"You were great," Kendra says.

"Thanks," I say with a big smile.

But then my smile disappears when I see Shelly start to straighten up Mrs. Sparrow's desk, too. I almost yell out that she's being a copycat, but I don't. Mrs. Sparrow might think I was being more like the Wicked Queen than Snow White.

When Shelly's done saying all her lines, guess what?

The whole class claps, that's what!

I don't like to admit it, but she did a very good job, too. Except for the copying part. That part still ruffles my whiskers.

During the rest of the tryouts, I keep my fingers crossed. I just hope that tomorrow when Mrs. Sparrow tells us which parts we get, that it's good news for me.

Chapter 5:

May the Best Cat Win

Most every day, I get sleepy after Mrs. Sparrow reads us a story. That's because the best time for a catnap is after story time. And a catnap is what I call one of my favorite things.

Only today, I don't get sleepy at all.

My tail is all twitchy and my ears are perked up. That's because Mrs. Sparrow is holding a list in her hands.

I, CatKid, know that list has the names of every kid in my class written on it. Also, I know it has all the roles in our class play written on it. But what I really want to know is *whose* name is written next to *which* role.

Thinking about that list makes me super purry!

"Mrs. Sparrow, I think CatKid is going to explode," Bradley says.

"Yeah, only know what? You would be purry, too, if you were one half cat like me," I say.

Mrs. Sparrow tells us both to settle down. But it's not so easy to settle down my cat half. No matter how hard I try, I can't stop purring.

"Pssst, CatKid," Maddie whispers. "I thought you might get a little overexcited, so I snuck this for you."

I look at her hand. She is holding a choc- olate chip cookie.

Chocolate chip cookies always settle me down.

"You're the best!" I whisper-shout and take the cookie. Maddie always knows just what I need.

I gobble it up in one bite.

Maddie giggles. She thinks that gobbling stuff is funny stuff. "Silly kitty," she says. I don't even mind that "silly kitty" name, because that's a funny name.

We stop giggling once Mrs. Sparrow clears her throat. She's ready to tell us which parts we got in the class play.

"I want you all to remember," she says, "even if you don't get the part you wanted, you're all still important to the play. There is no such thing as a small part."

Preston raises his hand and stands up. "What about the dwarves," he says. "Those are small parts."

The whole class laughs because that joke

cracks our heads up. Even Mrs. Sparrow smiles, so that's proof that it was one funny joke.

Once everyone is done laughing, Mrs. Sparrow reads the first seven names. One of those names is Maddie's name. "You will be the Seven Dwarfs," Mrs. Sparrow tells them.

Maddie is very happy to be a dwarf.

In fact, all the dwarves are happy! Even Preston is happy, and he's playing the dwarf who is grouchy all the time.

"I'm sorry you didn't get to be the prince," I whisper to him.

"That's okay with me," he says. "The prince has too many mushy parts, anyway."

"Yeah, those mushy parts are gross," I say. I'm sure glad I don't have to be the prince.

Next, Mrs. Sparrow tells Kendra she

gets to play the magic mirror. Kendra is a little sad she didn't get the Snow White part.

"But the magic mirror is a good part," Maddie says. "You get to wear a funny costume!"

Kendra smiles. She likes funny costumes.

"Now, for the part of Snow White," Mrs. Sparrow says. There are only two of us left who tried out for that part. One of them is me, CatKid, and the other is Shelly. I cross my fingers as tight as I can and close my eyes. "Please let it be me! Please let it be me! PLEASE! PLEASE!" I say. Only I say it in my head so that no one else can hear.

Only know what?

I was saying it so loud in my head that I didn't hear the name Mrs. Sparrow called, that's what.

"Who was it?" I asked when I open my eyes.

"It was *you*, tail-brain," Billy said.

"YIPPY! SKIPPY!" I shout. I'm so happy that I don't care about that tail-brain stuff. I leap straight up in the air. Then I grab my tail, spin around in a circle, and do my happy dance.

"Congratulations," Mrs. Sparrow says.

"You mean *cat*-gratulations!" I say right back.

Shelly stands up and raises her hand. "But what about me?" she asks. "Why didn't I get the part?"

I want to tell her it's because she's a copycat grumpy-pants, but my mom made me promise to be a good sport. So I don't say anything.

"You were also very good," Mrs. Sparrow tells Shelly. "That's why I need you to play another very important role."

"Really?" Shelly asks.

"Really," Mrs. Sparrow says. "I need you to play the Queen."

The whole class makes *oooohhhhs* and *aaaahhhhs*. It looks like Shelly is going to throw a temper tantrum.

But then I can't even believe my eyes, because Shelly smiles real proud.

"Why are you so happy?" Kendra asks her.

"Because the Queen is a more demanding role than silly Snow White," Shelly says in a snotty voice. "That means I'm the better actress."

I roll my eyes. Shelly *always* thinks she's better than everyone else!

Next it's the boys' turn to cross their fingers. That's because Mrs. Sparrow is going to tell them who gets to be Prince Charming.

"Who do you think it will be?" Maddie whispers.

I look around. "I don't know."

"Whoever it is, you'll have to pretend to be all mushy about them," Maddie says.

My eyes go all wide.

"I didn't think about that," I say.

I look around again and see Billy with his fingers crossed.

YIKES!

"Please don't let it be him! PLEASE! PLEASE!" I whisper to myself. Only guess what?

It doesn't work.

"Billy," Mrs. Sparrow says. "Congratulations, you got the part!"

I make a frowny face as Billy jumps up and down. "I'm a star! I'm a star!" he shouts.

Maybe being Snow White isn't so great. If I have to pretend to be mushy about Billy, this is going to be the hardest pretending I've ever done in my whole entire life!

Chapter 6:

A Real Live Kiss

"YUCK! YUCK! TRIPLE YUCK!" I shout as I read the last page of the play.

"What's the matter?" Maddie asks.

I point to the page and make a face like I'm feeling sick. "That's what!" I say.

Preston and Kendra read the page. We were all practicing our parts when I stopped practicing and started shouting.

"I don't see anything wrong." Preston says.

"Me, either," Kendra says.

"NOTHING WRONG? Are you blind?" I roar.

"It's right there," I tell them. "It says the prince wakes Snow White with a kiss. A real live kiss! That's the grossest thing I've ever heard!"

Maddie scratches her head. That's what she does when she's confused. "But CatKid, you wanted to be Snow White," she says. "Didn't you ever see the movie?"

I nod my head up and down.

"That part's in the movie," Kendra says.

"Yeah, only know what?" I say. "I always cover my eyes at the mushy part, so I didn't even know they kissed."

"But didn't you read the play when you practiced?" Maddie asks.

I make a frowny face. "I only practiced the first half," I tell them. I think that's because I was too busy with that cleaning-up stuff last night. I'll have to remember to tell her. If I catch boy cooties it will be all my mom's fault!

"Maybe it's only a pretend kiss," Kendra says.

I never thought of that. I clap my hands. "That won't be so bad. Even if it is Billy, at least it's only pretend. And you can't get cooties from a pretend kiss."

I start to feel better about the whole thing. But just then, I hear giggling coming from behind me. I turn my tail around and see Shelly standing there with her friend Olivia, who is in the other second-grade class.

"Yeah, and what's so funny?" I say.

"You and Billy," Shelly says.

"Yeah, once he kisses you, that means you're married!" Olivia says.

"*Everyone* knows that if you kiss a boy, that means you're married."

I look at
Maddie. "Is
that true?" I
whisper.

Maddie
shrugs.
"Um . . . I
think so."

"Told you so," Shelly says. Then she
and Olivia start making kissy noises
at me.

That's when I make growly noises
at them.

"Let's go," Olivia says.

"Yeah, before we get allergic to
CatKid," Shelly says with a laugh.

As they walk away, I don't have time to
be mad. That's because I have bigger fish
to worry about. Only, my problem has
nothing to do with fish, because fish are
yummy and kisses are yucky.

"What are you going to do?" Maddie asks.

"I don't know," I tell her. "But I have to stop that kiss and that's final."

I, CatKid, absolutely, positively do NOT want to marry Billy!

Chapter 7:

Grumpy Paws

When I come home from school, I drop my backpack by the door and take off my shoes. Then I go over to my favorite spot by the window. It's the sunshiniest spot in our whole house. And it's a cat fact that I like sunshiney spots.

Only today that spot doesn't make me happy. That's because I spent all afternoon trying to come up with a plan so that Snow White doesn't have to kiss Prince Charming.

I couldn't think of any.

That's why I cross my arms and sulk

when I sit down. That's what my dad calls *being a grumpy paws.*

"Hello kitten. I didn't hear you come in," my mom says when she sees me.

"Well I did come in," I tell her.

"I can see that," my mom says with a smile.

I don't smile back.

"How was school today?" my mom asks.

"Stinky!" I tell her. Then I finish my answer by sticking out my tongue and holding my nose.

My mom says that's not a very nice thing to say.

"But that's the truth," I tell her. "And you said a good CatKid always tells the truth, so there!" Then I make an extra grumpy face and sink down in the cushions.

My mom comes right over to my favorite spot and sits down next to me. She starts to scratch me behind the ears, but I don't go purry at all. Not like a lion, or a race car, or even a refrigerator.

"Is this about the class play?" my mom asks.

My ears perk right up!

"How did you know?" I ask. Sometimes I think my mom has super powers like they have in the cartoons. Because she always knows things that I'm thinking without me telling her.

"Moms just know," she says.

I wish I knew mom stuff. Then maybe I wouldn't have to study for spelling tests. I would just know the answers because that's what moms do.

"I'm sorry you didn't get the part you wanted," my mom says.

I scratch my head and look at her. Maybe moms don't know everything.

"Only know what?" I say. "I did get that part."

My mom claps her hands and gives me a hug. Then she shouts for my dad to come in, and she tells him all about it.

Then they both give me a double hug.

"I'm so proud of you," my dad says. "My little kitten is going to be a star."

I stop the hug right then and stand up.

"Yeah, only that's what's so stinky!" I tell them.

"I don't understand what you mean," my mom says.

"I mean, I get to be Snow White, but that's stinkier than not getting to be Snow White," I explain.

My mom and my dad give each other funny looks. Then they both shrug their shoulders. They still don't understand the stinky part of this whole business. Sometimes I wonder why grown-ups always need kids to explain simple stuff to them.

I, CatKid, take a deep breath.

Then I tell them the whole story.

"Once upon a time, this morning," I start, because that's the bestest way to start any story, "Mrs. Sparrow told us what part we got in the play. I was really, really, *really* hoping my name was the Snow White name. And it was! So I was happy, super happy, because that's what I always wanted."

"That doesn't sound bad at all," my dad says.

I make a huff.

"I'm getting to that part," I say.

"Sorry," my dad says. "Go on."

I take another deep breath and start where I left off. "Then Mrs. Sparrow called out a whole bunch of other stuff before she finally got to the prince. I crossed my fingers and hoped it wasn't Billy. But you know what? It was Billy!"

"Well, that doesn't sound so bad," my mom says.

I can't believe my ears!

"It's the yuckiest, most awfulest thing in the whole wide world!" I shout. "Billy's the worst prince ever! He's always mean to me. Plus now I have to kiss Billy in front of the whole school! And that means we're married forever and ever!"

My mom starts to giggle. Then my dad starts to giggle, too. But I, CatKid, don't think there is anything giggly about marrying Billy the Bully.

I stomp my foot and turn my back to them. That's called being *steamed and grumpy paws*.

But then my mom and dad both stop giggling. They come over and pat me on the head. "Don't worry, sweetie," my mom says. "It's just make believe."

"You and Billy won't be married," my dad says.

"Really?" I ask.

"Really," my dad says.

"And I can still be Snow White?" I ask.

"Of course," my mom says.

I put my finger to my chin. "You're not trying to trick me, are you?" I ask. Sometimes parents can be tricky. Like when they tell me we're going to get ice cream without telling me that we're going to the dentist first.

"Nope, no tricks," my dad says.

"Promise?" I ask.

"Promise," my dad says.

I start to feel not so grumpy anymore. Then my mom tells me we'll go shopping for a dress after dinner. She says I can get a new princess dress. I smile my whiskers. Thinking about my new dress makes me feel zero grumpy.

Maybe being the star of the play won't be so bad after all. But I'm still going to try my best to get out of kissing Billy. Because even if it doesn't mean we're married, I still don't want any of his gross cooties!

Chapter 8:

One Not-So-Lucky Cat

The day before our big play, my whole class can't even wait to be show-offs for our parents and friends. We're all super frisky, and it doesn't even matter that I'm the only one who is one whole-half cat!

For one whole week, our class has been getting ready for the play. We practiced our lines every afternoon. We even got to make props in art class. We colored a castle on a giant piece of cardboard and decorated our chairs and desks to look like furniture in the dwarves' house.

Maddie and I got to make fake trees out

of construction paper. We made four of them. That's called a forest.

And guess what?

They looked just like the real thing, that's what!

It's a cat-fact that this play is my new favorite subject in school. Plus, it keeps our class so busy that most kids forget to tease me about Billy.

But I helped a little bit with that.

That's because every time Mrs. Sparrow said it was time to practice the kissing part in the play, I would pretend to be sickish. I was only faking though. I didn't want to fake kiss Billy just in case my dad was wrong about that married stuff.

So Mrs. Sparrow always let us skip that part.

That makes me one lucky cat.

After story time, Mrs. Sparrow tells us she has another special announcement. "This afternoon we're going to have a dress rehearsal," she says.

Preston jumps up and raises his hand. "There is NO way I'm wearing a dress," he shouts. "Dresses are for girls!"

That makes all of us go giggly.

"You won't have to wear a dress," Mrs. Sparrow tells Preston. Preston wipes his forehead and takes a big breath.

Then I raise my hand real high and wave my tail around. "Yeah, only know what?" I say to Mrs. Sparrow. "I can't wait to wear my dress."

My dress is the prettiest!

My mom and I bought it at the fancy store in the mall. The lady who worked there asked me if I was going to a wedding. I made a huff at her. I had to tell her that me and Billy were only pretending to be mushy and that it was NOT a wedding.

"Nobody has to wear a dress, Dumb Ears!" Shelly says. "Dress rehearsal is just another name for practice."

Mrs. Sparrow gives Shelly a warning about the "Dumb Ears" stuff. She doesn't like name calling one little bit. But then she tells us that Shelly is sort of right and sort of wrong.

She says a dress rehearsal means we practice in our costumes. Only, she doesn't want us to bring our costumes to school until the actual play. "So for us, a dress rehearsal means that we will practice the play from start to finish, without stopping," Mrs. Sparrow explains.

"Not even once?" Kendra asks.

"Not even once," Mrs. Sparrow says.

I make a GULP, because start to finish means we'll have to practice the kissing part.

"But what if that's impossible?" Maddie asks.

"Yeah," I say. Then I give Maddie the thumbs-up, because that impossible stuff might work. There's no way we can practice the kissy stuff if it's impossible. That's a true fact.

"It's not impossible," Mrs. Sparrow says. "I've been watching you practice all week and I know you can do it."

I slump my shoulders. "Rats," I mumble.

"I guess that means you get to practice the cootie kiss," Shelly teases once Mrs. Sparrow tells us to go back to our desks. Then she sings the "CatKid and Billy, sitting in a tree, k-i-s-s-i-n-g" song.

"Yeah, only that's why you got the part of the Wicked Queen, so there!" I mutter.

Even when Shelly stops teasing, it doesn't make me feel any better. Because after this afternoon, every kid in my school is going to be singing that tree song!

Chapter 9:

Start to Finish

During the dress rehearsal, I, CatKid, stand on the stage and say my lines. Only I'm not even CatKid. That's because I'm Snow White. That's what acting is all about.

Just then, Maddie, Preston, and five other kids from my class walk onto the stage. Only they're acting, too. They are the seven dwarves.

"You're not children. You're little men," I say. Maddie and Lauren start to giggle. That's because the little men part is extra silly since they are girls.

"STOP!" Bradley shouts from the side

of the stage. His part in the play isn't really a part at all. Mrs. Sparrow calls his part *stage manager*.

I think stage manager is just a fancy name for bossy know-it-all. His job is to tell us when we make mistakes and to whisper lines to us if we forget them.

"There is no giggling at this part," he says.

"But I'm a smiley dwarf, so giggling is what I'm supposed to do," Maddie says.

"And I'm a silly dwarf," Lauren says. "And nothing is sillier than giggles."

"Yeah, so that means they're acting," I say.

"You can't act things that aren't in the play," Bradley says.

"It's okay, Bradley," Mrs. Sparrow says. "Let's keep going." Then she takes a big breath that blows her hair up in the air. It's the same kind of breath she made when Preston tripped over one of our fake trees. Plus, she made that same breath when Kendra made the mirror stick out its tongue at Shelly.

Sometimes my mom makes that breath, too. She calls it *being frazzled*.

I, Snow White, am not frazzled at all. At least not until we get to the part after I pretend to eat the poison apple.

The apple part is fine. It's my favorite part. I get to spin around and moan and tumble to the floor. Then the curtain goes down and I hurry backstage before the next part. That next part is the one that makes my stomach go funny.

"*Pssst*, Maddie," I say backstage. "Do you think Mrs. Sparrow will be mad if I don't do this part?"

Maddie makes her eyes all big. Then she nods her head up and down.

"You have to do this part," Maddie says. "You're Snow White!"

"But what about the kiss," I whisper real quiet so no one else can hear.

Maddie scratches her head. Then she points in the air. "I know," she says. "Just cover your mouth like this." Then she covers her mouth with both hands. She says if Billy kisses my hands then it's not really a kiss.

I'm not so sure, but I tell her I'll try, anyway.

So I climb on the table that is supposed to be Snow White's bed and pretend to be in a deep sleep. That's because the poison apple makes Snow White hibernate until she is kissed.

"Ready?" Bradley asks.

"Ready," I say, but it's a lie. I'm only acting ready.

The curtain goes up and I close my eyes. Only I don't close them all the way. I peek a little so that I can see Billy.

He walks across the stage and says a bunch of stuff about true love. By the time he comes over to my bed, I can hear the other kids laughing.

I open my eyes and see Billy staring at me.

Then he makes a kissy face.

I cover my mouth with both hands.

I know I'm supposed to wait until Billy kisses me to sit up, but I sit up, anyway.

"CUT!" I yell. I learned that on TV. It means everyone has to stop acting.

"What's the matter CatKid?" Mrs. Sparrow asks.

"Um . . . well, I don't think Billy should kiss me because I feel a little sick-ish," I say. Then I act a whole bunch of fake sneezes.

"Yeah, me, too," Billy says. Then he does that fake sneezing thingy, too.

Mrs. Sparrow makes her frazzled face again. "Okay, okay," she says. "Just start again from after the kiss."

I smile real wide.

So does Billy, because he doesn't even want to be married, either. That makes us the teeniest, tiniest bit friends.

We both say our last two lines and the rest of the class claps their hands. The dress rehearsal is over!

Mrs. Sparrow tells us all that we did a good job. Then she reminds everybody to remember their costumes tomorrow. "And practice your lines tonight," she says. "We want everything to be perfect."

The whole class cheers.

Only when I cheer, it's for pretend because if everything is going to be perfect, that means no getting out of the mushy stuff.

Chapter 10:

Plan B

At the end of the school day, all the kids in my class go to their bus. But I stay in my classroom.

I have an idea to fix the play problem. That's what I call Plan B, and I need to talk to Mrs. Sparrow about it.

If something needs fixing, you have to go to the top. So I, CatKid, am going to the tippy-top. I'm going above the mayor and even the president, and straight to my teacher.

I get up from my desk and march over to hers. Only when I get up there, I get a little bit scared. So my voice comes out whispery all by itself.

"Mrs. Sparrow?" I say.

Mrs. Sparrow looks up from her desk. Then she smiles at me. That makes me feel not scared anymore, and I smile back. "What's on your mind, CatKid?" she asks.

I reach up and put my hands on my head. I even roll my eyes up and try to look up there, but I can't see anything. "Um, I don't think there's anything on my mind," I tell her.

"It's just an expression," Mrs. Sparrow says.

I make a frown. I don't like that expression because it tricked me into patting my head. Plus, it doesn't make any sense.

"What did you want to ask me?" Mrs. Sparrow asks.

"Oh yeah," I say. Then I remember my idea. "Do you think maybe it would be

better if instead of a kiss, the Prince gives Snow White a pony to wake her up from hibernation?"

Then I smile my whiskers because that pony stuff is good stuff.

"Why do you think that would be better?" Mrs. Sparrow asks me.

I throw my arms out to the side. That's the easiest question a teacher has ever asked me. "Because everyone wants a pony," I say. "And NO ONE wants a yucky kiss!"

Then I wipe my mouth to show her just how yucky kisses are.

Only know what?

Mrs. Sparrow goes all giggly, that's what!

If I weren't afraid of going to the principal's office, I would almost make a huff at her. How come grown-ups never understand that this kissing business is serious business?

But then Mrs. Sparrow stops laughing. "Is that what's been bothering you all week? Is that why you haven't wanted to practice the end of the play?" she asks.

I nod my head up and down and down and up.

"It's only for pretend," she says. "You don't really have to kiss Billy."

"I don't?" I ask.

"Not if you don't want to," she says.

"And then I won't get cooties and won't have to be married to Billy for my whole life?" I ask.

"Absolutely, positively not," Mrs. Sparrow says with a smile.

"YIPPY!" I shout. Then I grab my tail and do my happy dance all over the place.

"I will tell Billy about it tomorrow," she says. "I have a funny feeling he might be happy about it, too." Then she tells me to hurry so I don't miss my bus.

"Thanks! You're the best teacher ever!" I shout. Then I race out the door and right onto my bus. I can't wait to tell Maddie the good news. Plan B was a perfect success.

Chapter 11:

Action!

Backstage, I can hear the crowd. The whole school is in the auditorium to watch our class play. Plus, the parents of the kids in my class are here, too.

My mom and dad are here. They came to my classroom to wish me luck. That made me happy, except that they called me "kitten" in front of my friends.

But right now, I don't care about that kitten stuff. That's because Principal Wheeler is talking to the audience, and he tells them the play is going to start any minute.

I, CatKid, am a little bit of a fraidy cat

about it. That part is a secret though. I wouldn't want anyone to know.

Only know what?

Maddie always knows my secrets. That's the job of a best friend.

"What's the matter?" Maddie whispers to me. She knows something is the matter whenever my tail goes all bushy like a squirrel's tail.

Right now, my tail is as bushy as two squirrels put together! It looks like the fake beard Maddie is wearing.

"I'm worried I might forget my lines," I whisper to Maddie.

Maddie tells me not to worry. "You were great in practice," she says. "Plus, smarty-pants Bradley will whisper any lines you forget."

"But what if my tail doesn't stop being bushy?" I ask. "Whoever heard of a princess cat with a bushy tail?"

"Whoever heard of a princess *cat* in the first place," Shelly says. She snuck up behind us and spied on everything we said.

"Besides, you should be more worried about kissing Billy than your silly tail."

My mom says princesses don't stick their tongues out at people, but I don't care. I stick my tongue out at Shelly.

"Anyway," I say, "Mrs. Sparrow says it's only for pretend, so that doesn't count."

"What if she was fibbing?" Shelly says.

"Teachers don't fib," Maddie says.

"Yeah," I say. "Why would she fib?"

"Duh?" Shelly says. "Maybe she fibbed so you'd keep your eyes closed instead of messing up the last scene like in rehearsal?"

I scratch my head.

Maddie scratches her fake beard.

Sometimes Mrs. Sparrow can be tricky. One time she tricked me into doing a math problem by telling me it was a cookie problem. I added up those cookies not knowing it was a trick.

Maybe Shelly is right. Maybe this is another trick. Maybe I really will have to be Mrs. Princess Billy Charming my whole entire life.

YUCK!

"Here comes your boyfriend," Shelly teases when Billy walks over to us.

"Um . . . CatKid," Billy says.

"What?" I say back.

"My mom told me to tell you that you look . . . not so icky," he says. Then his face turns all red and he hurries away.

Shelly laughs just like the Wicked Queen. "Told you so," she teases. "Billy and CatKid sitting in a tree." I growl at her as she goes on stage.

When the curtain goes up, I, CatKid, not only have a bushy tail, but my face is also bright red. I'm starting to wish my class never got picked to do this play stuff.

Chapter 12:

To Kiss Or Not To Kiss?

If there's one thing I know about cats, it's that cats love being the center of attention. I, CatKid, love being the center of attention, too. That's why once the play starts, I forget all about the stinky stuff that happened backstage.

My tail stops being bushy.

My face stops being red.

And another thing, I don't forget any of my lines. Not counting the lines I was supposed to say into the wishing well, or the ones when I was supposed to tell the dwarves about the Wicked Queen. Besides those lines, I forget zero of my lines.

And guess what?

Every time I act something, all those kids watching clap like crazy, that's what!

It's not just me, either. They like the whole play. They get especially giggly whenever the dwarves come on stage. Those dwarves sure are funny. Even I get giggly when Lauren sneezes so hard her beard comes off.

AHH-CHOO

It was just like Mrs. Sparrow said. The play was going perfectly.

Then I get to my poison apple part. "I feel . . . dizzy," I say. Then I spin around in circles before KABOOM!

I fall right on my tail, just like the play says.

Shelly's dressed up like an old woman and she laughs. Her laugh sounds really

mean and scary. The audience claps, only
I want to tell them that Shelly isn't even
acting. She always laughs that way!

The curtain comes down and I stand
up and hurry off the stage.

"Nice job, girls," Mrs. Sparrow says.

"Thanks," we say back.

"You were great," Maddie says.

I smile my whiskers real wide. Only
then, I hear Mrs. Sparrow tell the other
kids to bring the Snow White bed onto
the stage.

I stop smiling and make a GULP!

I was having so much fun acting that I forgot I was supposed to be worrying.

"*Pssst*! CatKid, you have to go out there," Maddie whispers.

"Yeah, I know," I say. "Only, my feet don't want to work." If Mrs. Sparrow is fibbing to me, then I, CatKid, will be married to the grossest tail-pulling bully in the school!

"You *have* to. It's the rules," Preston says.

I shake my head. "N-O!" I say.

Shelly comes up and crosses her arms. "Get on stage, Dumb Ears!" she shouts at my face. "My grandparents drove three hours to get here. I'm not going to let you ruin the whole play!"

I, CatKid, do not want to ruin the whole play.

But I also don't want to pretend to be mushy.

"It'll be fine," Maddie says. "Just remember to cover your mouth."

"Are you sure?" I ask.

"Sure I'm sure!" Maddie says, and best friends never tell fibs, so I know I can trust her.

"Okay," I mumble.

I walk onto the stage and climb up on the bed. Then I close my eyes real tight. Plus, I cross my fingers really, really, really tight.

The spotlight shines on me as soon as the curtain goes up. I can hear Billy walk onto the stage.

"There she is," he says. "I wonder if she is the same girl I lost my heart to so long ago."

I make an icky face even though I'm supposed to be asleep. Then Billy walks over to me. I peek with one eye as he leans closer.

He makes a kissy face.

That proves it. Mrs. Sparrow was fibbing!

I sit right up in that bed!

THUMP!

My head and Billy's head bump together.

"Ouch!" Billy says, rubbing his forehead.

"Ouch, right back," I say and rub my forehead.

The audience doesn't say anything. That's because they are too busy laughing. "You still need to kiss," Bradley whispers from the side of the stage. Billy closes his eyes. He makes another kissy face.

I quickly cover my mouth with both hands just in time.

I can't believe it! Billy kissed my hand!

"YUCK!" I shout. I wipe my hands on my dress to get any boy cooties off. "What did you do that for?" I ask.

Billy doesn't answer. He's too busy wiping girl cooties from his mouth.

"Say your last lines," Bradley says.

We say them, only it doesn't matter because the crowd is laughing so hard they can't hear. The play is absolutely, positively RUINED!

Chapter 13:

A Star Is Born

I make a grumpy face at Billy as the curtain comes down. "It was supposed to be for pretend!" I yell at him. I wipe my hands off one more time just to be safe.

"I was pretending!" Billy yells back. "You're the one who sat up and bumped me in the head. I get confused when I get bumped in the head!"

"Maybe you should get a new head," I tell him.

"Maybe I wouldn't have to if you weren't such a clumsy cat!" Billy tells me.

I make a very loud growl at him.

That's when Mrs. Sparrow comes over to us.

I frown and put my head down. "I'm sorry I messed up the play," I tell her. "But it's all Billy's fault. He kissed me for real when he wasn't supposed to!"

"It's not my fault," Billy says.

"Is too," I say.

"No one messed up anything," Mrs. Sparrow says.

I scratch my head.

"That doesn't make sense," I say. "We didn't say the lines right. That means we messed up."

Mrs. Sparrow smiles. She tells me to listen to the crowd on the other side of the curtain. I  perk up my cat ears and listen.

That crowd is cheering like crazy.

"They loved it," Mrs. Sparrow says. "And that's all that matters."

"Really?" I ask.

"Really!" Mrs. Sparrow says. "You two are the stars of the show."

I look at Billy and Billy looks at me. We smile really big. It feels good to be the stars of the show. Plus, we're not even married because I covered my mouth. Those are the rules.

"Everybody back on stage!" Bradley shouts. "We have to take a bow." Bows are how the audience knows it's time to thank the stars of the play.

Billy and I rush out to the center of the stage. All the other kids in my class come out, too. I see Maddie and wave. She waves back.

"Good job," she says.

"Good job yourself," I say.

Then the curtain goes up and I can see

the whole school standing up and clapping. I even see my mom and dad, so I
wave. They wave back. I can't even wait to
give them a hug.

First, though, we have to take a bow.

We all hold hands and bend down.
Then we stand back up again and those
people clap even louder.

Just then, I look down and notice that
Billy is still holding my hand. He notices,
too. We both let go super quick and start
to wipe the cooties off. That makes the

laughing start all over again as the curtain comes down.

I, CatKid, still don't know what's so funny about all that mushy stuff, but it doesn't even matter. I still love being the star of the show. So I blow kisses to the clapping people, because that's what stars do. And that's the kind of mushy stuff I like.